W9-AOX-227

For Marco
Jung-Hee Spetter

For Shana, Jan and Mas
Anke Kranendonk

Library of Congress Cataloging-in-Publication Data

Kranendonk, Anke.
 [Ik kom zo! English]
 Just a minute / Anke Kranendonk : pictures by Jung-Hee Spetter.
  p. cm.
 Summary: Neglected by his busy mother, Piggy wreaks havoc both
inside and outside the house.
 ISBN 1-886910-29-4 (alk. paper)
 [1. Behavior—Fiction. 2. Pigs—Fiction.] I. Spetter, Jung-Hee,
1969- ill. II. Title
PZ7.K85935Ju 1998
[E]—dc21   97-32649

Copyright © 1998 by Lemniscaat b.v. Rotterdam
Originally published in the Netherlands under the title *Ik kom zo!* by Lemniscaat b.v. Rotterdam
All rights reserved
Printed and bound in Belgium
Firts American edition

Just a minute!

Anke Kranendonk

Pictures by
Jung-Hee Spetter

Front Street ⅋ Lemniscaat

Asheville, North Carolina

Island Library
4077 Main Street
Chincoteague, VA 23336

"Mommy, will you read me a book?
"Not right now, dear. In just a minute.

"Now, Mommy?"
"I can't. Go inside and I'll be in soon."

"Yoo-hoo! Mommy!"
"I'm almost done."

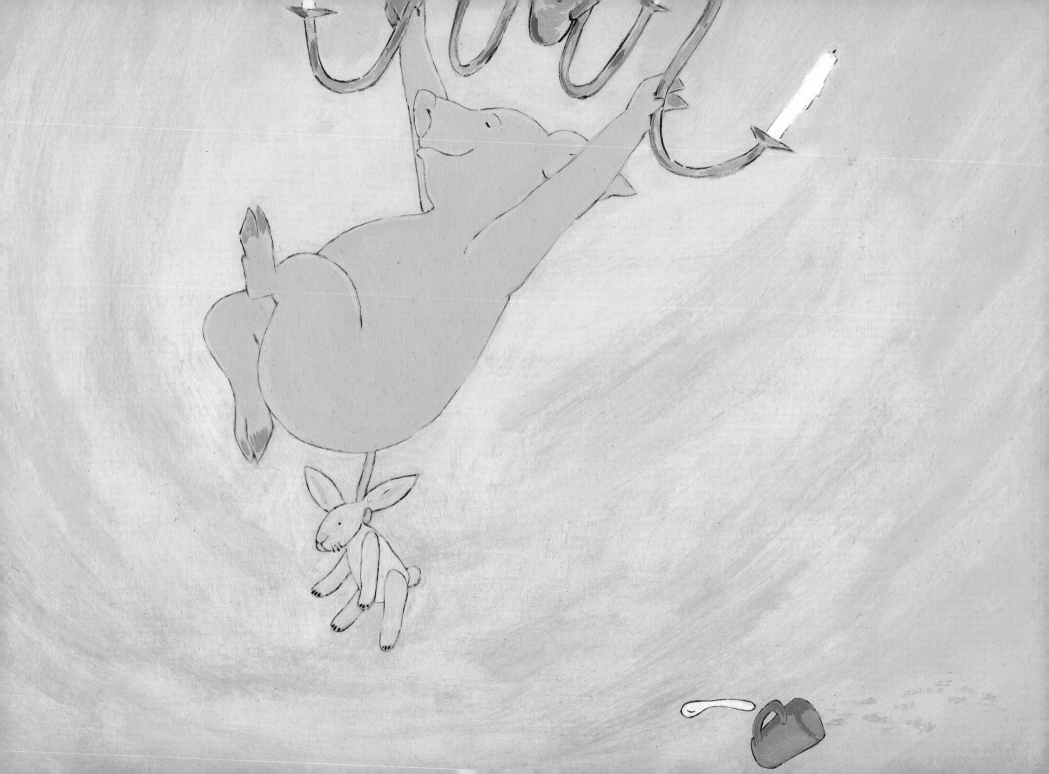

"Mommy! Look."
"Just a second, dear."

"Mommy, come play with me.
"Soon, dear.

"Mommy, can you help me now?

"Just one more second.

"Phew! Piggy, I'm finished."

"Piggy, where are you?"

"Piggy."

"Piggy?"

"Piggy!"

"Here I am, Mommy. I'll be done in just a minute."